Animals
in a
Zoo Parade

Dennis Wilson

Illustrated by Frances Espanol.

To order additional copies of this book, contact:
Xlibris
844-714-8691
www.Xlibris.com
Orders@Xlibris.com

ISBN: Softcover   978-1-6641-5497-1
        EBook   978-1-6641-5496-4

Print information available on the last page

Rev. date: 01/26/2021

This is dedicated to children and parents
who enjoyed poetry with a message.

Polly Parrot had a thought of an animal parade
All with different costumes that would be displayed

A parade of the animals! "Here's what we want to do"
Said Polly Parrot to the monkey and the kooky kangaroo

"We'll get a brand new look with wigs and shoes and clothes
No one will ever know us with outfits that we chose"

The animals were so excited they ran back to the zoo
To find new duds to wear, their old image will never do

ZOO

WELCOME TO OUR PARADE

When all the animals were dressed they gathered to parade
With their brand new costumes that they had made

Frankie Frog placed frosting on his funny face

Lady Lion looked lavish with her lovely legged lace

Wilhelmina Walrus wore a wilted worn-out wig

Freddy Fox wore flip flops and danced an Irish jig

Shiny silver sequins clung to Stinky Sammy Skunk

Dumbo swayed in the parade with a decorated trunk

In spite of the costume change they were unaware
That in a zoo parade the children really did not care

For children love each animal as a unique creation
And see no sense in dressing to form a new sensation

ZOO

So the animals all went back to the zoo once more
And returned to the same old way as they looked before

ZOO

Polly Parrot reminds us to always be aware
And never dress outrageous even on a dare

For like all the animals we must take special care
To always be ourselves no matter what we wear.

Printed in the United States
By Bookmasters